THE AMAZING SPIDER-MAN™

The MOVIE STORYBOOK

ADAPTED BY
MICHAEL SIGLAIN

JAMES VANDERBILT

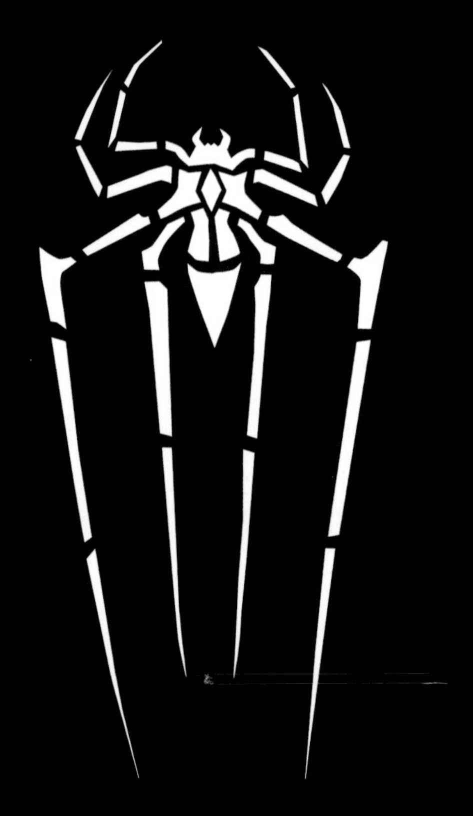

Printed in the United States of America

First Edition

WHEN THE GLASS SHATTERED, PETER PARKER RAN AS FAST AS HE COULD. He had been creeping around the house, silently looking for his father's hiding spot, but not anymore. Their games of hide-and-seek were always fun, but the sound of the glass breaking from the rainstorm outside had frightened Peter. Now, he didn't just want to find his father, he wanted to make sure that everything was okay.

PETER RAN INTO HIS FATHER'S STUDY, a room that was usually off-limits. Peter looked around at the large wooden desk and spotted a case that contained various species of spider. Then Peter saw a large spider—one unlike any he had ever seen before—suspended inside a bell jar on his dad's desk. The spider was long dead, but it still sent a shiver down Peter's spine.

Just then, Peter's dad rushed into the room. He seemed to be bothered by something. But rather than explaining why he was in such a hurry, Peter's dad picked up his son and quickly exited the house. Peter didn't even have time to put on his shoes!

Inside the car, Peter learned that he and his parents were going to his uncle and aunt's house in Forest Hills, Queens. Peter's eyes moved from his parents and settled on his dad's briefcase. It had the initials RP, for Richard Parker, embossed on its leather shell.

Peter's dad pulled a colorful object from the briefcase and handed it to his son. It was a Rubik's Cube. Peter loved puzzles, and this one instantly took his mind off the fact that his parents had fled their home as if their lives depended on it.

PETER STOOD IN THE HALLWAY AND WATCHED as Aunt May and Uncle Ben spoke with his parents. His mom seemed sad as she told May, "He'll only drink chocolate milk. And he doesn't like crust on his sandwiches and—"

Then Peter's father leaned down to talk to him. "You're going to be staying with Aunt May and Uncle Ben for a little while," Peter's father began. "There is something your mom and I need to do. I need you to be a good boy."

Peter's dad then changed the subject. "I was hiding in the coatroom. Off the hall," he said, referring to their earlier game of hide-and-seek.

"I don't like that room," Peter said.

"That's why I hid there," Peter's father replied. "That's the secret to the game. Remember that. Be good, Peter."

Then Peter's dad handed his briefcase to his brother, Ben, hugged Peter tightly, and walked out into the rain.

"It's all right. Everything's going to be all right," Aunt May said reassuringly to Peter, who stared out into the stormy night and watched the car pull away.

THAT WAS THE LAST TIME PETER PARKER SAW HIS PARENTS.

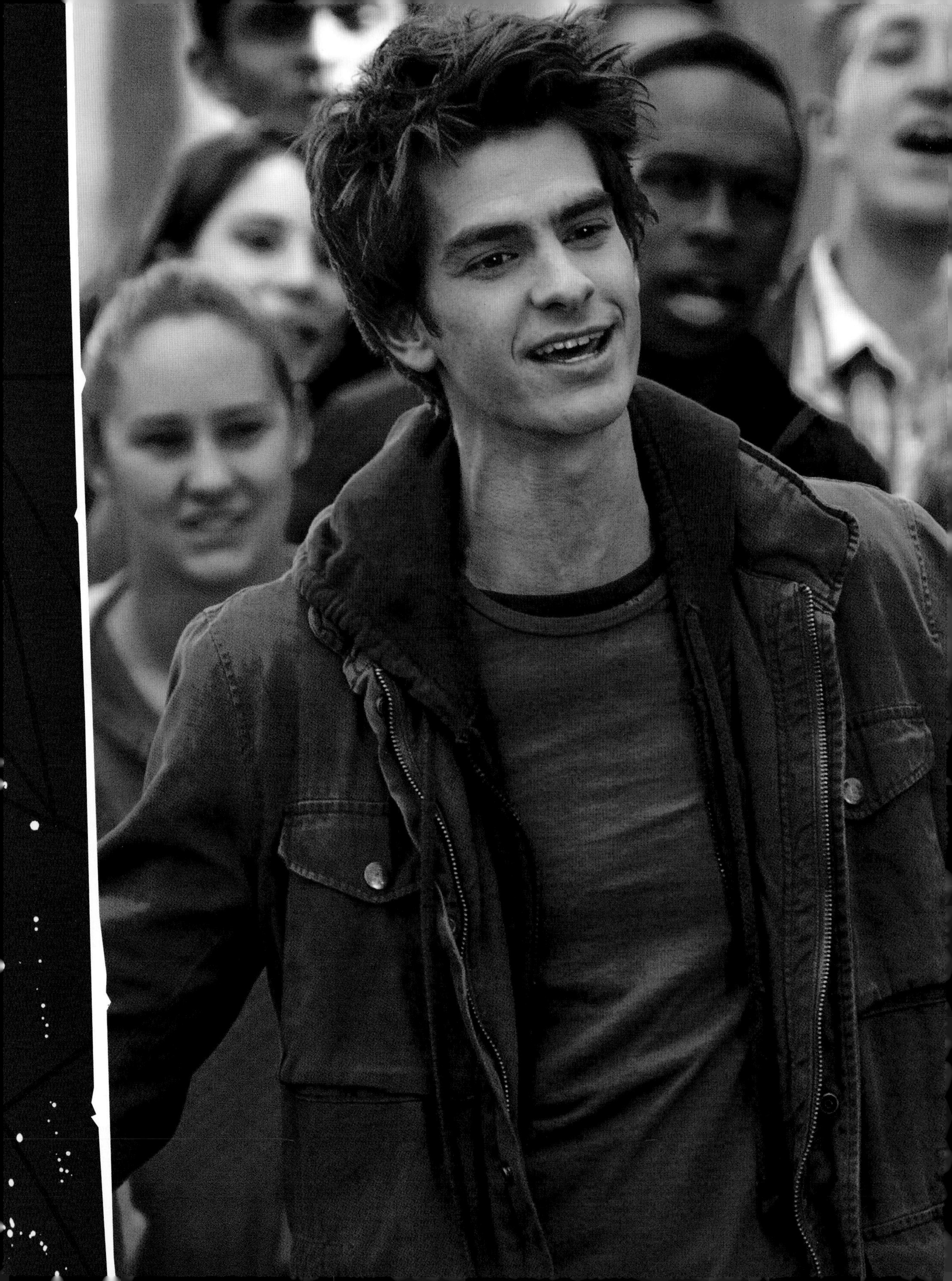

PETER PARKER WALKED DOWN THE HALLS of Midtown Science High School with a camera in his hand. Peter was the school's best photographer, and his pictures had captured everything from the football team to the chess club.

Peter's lens was currently fixed on cheerleader and debate-club captain Gwen Stacy, who was sitting alone, her face buried in a book. As Peter raised his camera, Gwen lowered her book, allowing Peter to catch a glimpse of her beautiful, radiant face. Peter quickly snapped a picture, but was then distracted by a commotion in the cafeteria.

"Eat your vegetables, Gordon," said Flash Thompson, Midtown Science High's resident bully. Flash was holding Gordon by his ankles just above a plate of spaghetti. Peter knew he had to do something.

"Put him down, Flash," Peter interjected. Peter tried to get the rowdy crowd to help Gordon. "I think he deserves better than being force-fed meatballs while being dangled upside down, don't you?"

But the crowd wasn't on Peter's side. They chanted for Gordon to eat. Peter had to resort to drastic measures.

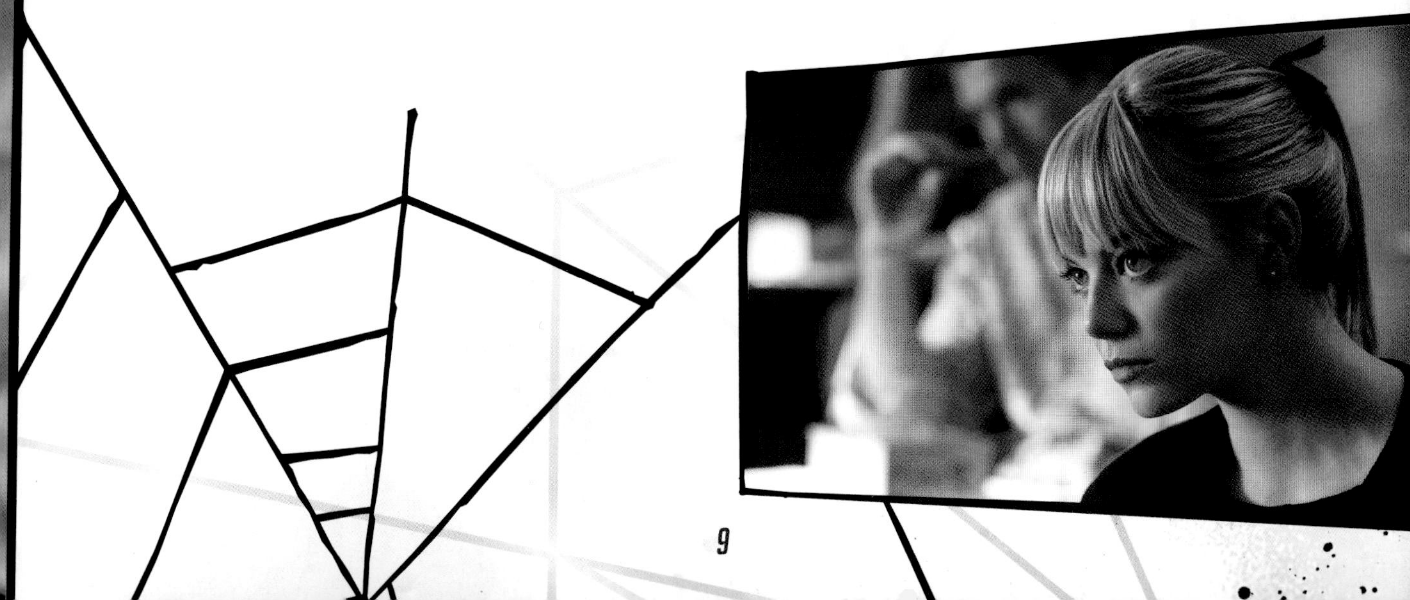

"PUT. HIM. DOWN," Peter said, before pausing for effect to add, "Eugene."

Flash Thompson hated many things, but most of all, he hated being called by his proper first name. Flash dropped Gordon into his spaghetti and cracked Peter across the jaw with a mighty blow.

Then the captain of the football team hit Peter again and again until Peter finally gave up. After the crowd dispersed, Peter realized his camera had been broken in the fight. But it was too late to think about that now—Peter was late for class.

A bruised and battered Peter Parker found a seat behind Gwen Stacy in chemistry class.

"I thought it was great what you did," Gwen began. "But you should probably go to the school nurse. You might have a concussion."

Peter was transfixed. He couldn't believe Gwen was actually talking to him. But when she asked him his name, he felt a sudden disappointment. "We've been going to school together for ten years," Peter protested.

"I know your name," Gwen said. "I want to see if *you* know it."

"Peter. Parker," he stammered. Gwen smiled, then turned her attention back toward the teacher.

"Gwen Stacy knows my name," Peter said aloud to himself.

"I can hear you," Gwen replied.

WHEN PETER RETURNED HOME, Uncle Ben asked him to help out in the basement. The refrigerator was broken and leaking water, but Peter could not fix it until he had the proper hardware. So instead, he helped Uncle Ben move and sort boxes. In one of the boxes, Peter found an old leather briefcase with the initials RP embossed on the front. It was his father's briefcase!

Peter took his newfound treasure to his room to examine it more closely. It contained a pair of his father's glasses, some fountain pens, a piece of an old newspaper clipping, and a photograph of Peter's mother, Mary Parker.

Peter then noticed the Rubik's Cube on his shelf from the night his parents left. He thought about the puzzle, then twisted and turned the briefcase as if it, too, was a puzzle to unlock. It was. Peter found a secret folder filled with scientific formulas.

PETER THEN PUT ON HIS FATHER'S GLASSES and looked at himself in the mirror. He was the spitting image of his dad. At that moment, Uncle Ben walked into the room. Peter quickly took off the glasses.

Uncle Ben explained that the person in the newspaper clipping was none other than brilliant scientist Dr. Curt Connors. "Your father worked with him," Uncle Ben said. "But after *that* night . . . he never called. Not once."

Later, Peter went online to learn more about Dr. Connors. He was an award-winning scientist at Oscorp, and Peter decided that he would pay him a visit in the morning.

PETER STOOD INSIDE THE MASSIVE OSCORP TOWER LOBBY and wondered how he was going to get by their security and get in to see Dr. Connors. Taking a deep breath, he approached the pretty receptionist in an attempt to talk his way in. Happily, the receptionist mistook him for an Oscorp intern.

Peter quickly reached out and grabbed the first intern badge he could find, pinned it to his shirt, and proceeded to mix in with the rest of the interns. Suddenly, the silhouette of a beautiful young girl holding a clipboard caught their attention. Peter gulped as the girl came into view—it was Gwen Stacy!

"Welcome to Oscorp," Gwen said as she introduced herself. "I'm the head intern for Dr. Connors, and I'll be taking you on your tour." Not wanting to be noticed, Peter made his way to the back of the group as the tour began.

Soon, they were on the forty-second floor, visiting the animal-dynamics lab, and Dr. Curt Connors. Connors was engaging and intelligent—and also missing his right arm. He informed the group that he was hard at work on a cure to regrow his missing limb, and asked his audience how to go about doing such a thing. No one answered.

That's when Peter spoke up. "Cross-species genetics," he said.

With that, both Connors and Gwen turned their attention to Peter Parker, currently masquerading as intern Rodrigo Guevara.

OSCORP
INDUSTRIES
OSCORP

DR. CONNORS WAS INSTANTLY IMPRESSED WITH PETER, and the two started a scientific debate right then and there. It was only when Connors's phone started ringing that he cut short their discussion and returned to work. And that's when Gwen blocked Peter's path.

"Rodrigo . . . *hola,*" she said threateningly. She thought Peter was following her—so Peter accused *her* of following *him*. The two argued, then started to flirt—until Gwen realized she had to get back to the other interns. That's when Peter snuck away. . . .

An awestruck Peter walked through the laboratory. Soon, he was able to sneak into one particularly impressive lab. The room seemed to float and shimmer. When Peter looked around, he saw that the walls were actually made of spiderwebs and that a sleek, spiderlike contraption was gathering these delicate strands and weaving them into one single web-line.

At the sound of a lab tech outside, Peter whirled around, accidentally knocking into some of the webs and causing two dozen small spiders to drop onto his head, then spill onto his neck and shoulders.

PETER FROZE AND DID HIS BEST NOT TO SCREAM.

PETER COULDN'T TAKE IT ANY LONGER. He did a mad dance to shake off the spiders and raced out of the lab, almost knocking over the technicians who were waiting just outside the door.

Thinking he was safe, Peter ran into the nearest elevator, only to come face-to-face with Gwen Stacy. "Give it to me," Gwen ordered.

Peter was caught off-guard. Then he realized she was talking about his intern badge. As he handed it over, Peter didn't notice a spider from the lab crawling around the back of his neck.

Just as Gwen left the elevator, the spider bared its fangs and dug them into Peter's neck. "Ow!" Peter yelled.

Gwen eyed Peter suspiciously as he ran his hand over his neck. There was a small welt, but nothing else.

THE SPIDER WAS GONE.

OSCORP

PETER SAT, HALF ASLEEP, INSIDE A NYC SUBWAY CAR,

completely oblivious to the group of men and women who were coming toward him. They looked as if they had just come from a big football game, but Peter was too dazed to pay any attention to them.

Upon seeing him, one of the guys balanced a bottle on top of Peter's head. Just as a drop of condensation trickled down the bottle and onto Peter's cheek, Peter awoke with a jolt.

In less than a second, Peter swatted the bottle away and scurried up the side of the subway car, momentarily sticking to the ceiling. One of the girls looked up in shock. "Did you see that?" she said to her friend. Then, turning to Peter, she began, "How did you—?"

But by then Peter was already back on the ground. He put his hand on the girl's shoulder in an attempt to calm her down, but his hand stuck to her jacket. When he tried to move it, he accidentally ripped her jacket clean off. That's when everyone went after Peter!

PETER JUMPED OUT OF THE WAY of the attack as if it was suddenly second nature! Then he weaved and dodged between the men, avoiding every punch and kick like an expert. He was nimble and precise. For the first time, Peter Parker actually won a fight.

As if signaling the end of a boxing match, the subway chimed and the conductor announced that the train was at its last stop: Coney Island. That's when Peter realized just how long he had been on the train. He was supposed to get off several stops ago—in Queens, not Brooklyn!

When the subway doors opened, Peter apologized to the crowd and dashed away into the night. He then ran twenty-seven miles back to Aunt May and Uncle Ben's house.

"I'm sorry. I know I'm late. Irresponsible. Insensitive . . . I'm hungry," Peter said as he walked through the door. He then proceeded to raid the fridge. He started with leftover meat loaf and moved on to chicken, cole slaw, apple pie, and ice cream!

JUST BEFORE A STUFFED PETER was about to go to bed, he regarded himself in his bedroom mirror. He didn't know how he did all those fantastic things on the subway, but he sure looked like the same old Peter Parker.

And then he saw it: a thin thread of silk lay trembling across his throat. The silk was delicate but impressively strong. Peter followed the line from his throat down past his shoulder and finally into his shirt pocket. He lifted the line from his pocket and saw, tethered to the line but obviously dead, a spider. But not just any spider, a spider that resembled the one he saw back in his father's office when he was a kid.

Peter studied the creature intently, then looked back at himself in the mirror. While he didn't say it out loud, Peter Parker knew that his life would be forever changed from that moment on.

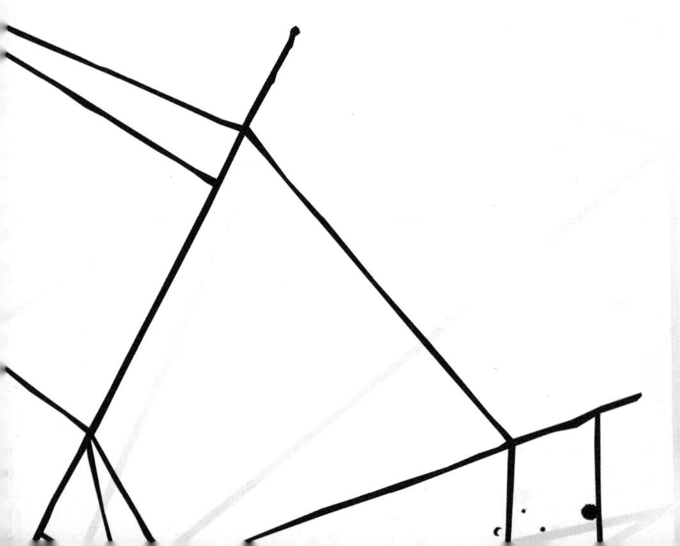

A LOUD BBRRIINNNGGG FROM PETER'S ALARM clock jolted him awake. Instinctively, Peter reached out his arm to stop the ringing. But instead of turning off the alarm, Peter shattered it!

Peter went to the one spot where he suddenly felt comfortable: the roof. Peter sat there dangling his legs and thinking about his father, the spider bite, and his new almost-superhuman abilities.

"How in blazes did you get up there?" Uncle Ben said from the front porch, breaking Peter out of his thoughts.

"Oh . . . I climbed," Peter said truthfully. Uncle Ben just shook his head and walked back inside to Aunt May.

Over the next few days, Peter learned how to better use and control his newfound abilities. He found himself stronger, faster, and more agile than he had ever been before.

BUT PETER WAS PREOCCUPIED WITH THESE POWERS and began to disregard Aunt May and Uncle Ben. One night, when Peter forgot to walk Aunt May home from the store, Uncle Ben got very cross with him.

Peter stormed out of the house because of the argument with his uncle, and then tragedy struck. When Peter returned home, he learned that a crook had killed Uncle Ben, who had gone out looking for Peter. Aunt May was devastated and Peter was guilt-stricken. If only he had been there, maybe he could've saved his uncle.

That's when Peter decided to use his powers for good. But he couldn't run around as Peter Parker. He needed a disguise . . . a costume. So he took his inspiration from a wrestling poster . . . and from the creature that gave him his amazing powers.

HE WOULD BECOME SPIDER-MAN!

ONE NIGHT, AFTER PETER TRIED TO STOP some local thugs, he returned home much later than expected and found Aunt May waiting up for him.

"Where have you been?" Aunt May asked, but Peter couldn't tell his aunt that he was out fighting crime as the Amazing Spider-Man. "Did you remember the eggs?" she asked.

Peter had forgotten all about the eggs that she had asked him to bring home. Aunt May was very disappointed in him.

And then Peter realized Aunt May was upset about more than just the eggs. Aunt May was sad over Uncle Ben. She missed him.

"I can't sleep," she told Peter. "Do you know what it's like to be alone after thirty-eight years?"

Peter had no response. He felt terrible for his aunt. He knew that he would make it up to her. He wouldn't let Aunt May down again.

PETER'S FAMILY LIFE MIGHT HAVE BEEN BAD, but his social life was getting better. To his disbelief, Peter had been invited to have dinner with Gwen Stacy and her family; now he sat at the dining room table in a state of temporary shock. To one side of him was the girl of his dreams, Gwen Stacy. And to every other side was her family, including her three brothers and her parents. And if Peter wasn't intimidated enough, Gwen's father was also a captain in the New York City Police Department, tasked with finding the masked man who dressed like a spider.

"So tell us a little about yourself, Peter," Gwen's mom asked.

"Not really much to tell," Peter responded nervously.

"In my line of work, that's a dead giveaway that a man has something to hide," Captain Stacy said.

To quickly change the subject, one of Gwen's brothers asked his father if the police had caught the "Spider-Guy" yet. "No, but he's an amateur," Captain Stacy began. "And I just assigned two of my best detectives to the case."

"I think most people would say that he's providing a public service," Peter said, worried. "It looks like he's trying to help."

But Captain Stacy wasn't going to let Peter—or Spider-Man—off the hook. "Whose side are you on? Do you know something we don't?"

AND THAT'S WHEN GWEN STEPPED IN. "Peter's not your enemy, Daddy," she said, though it made little difference to the captain.

Gwen then excused herself. Peter thanked them all for a delicious dinner and followed Gwen out of the living room and up onto the building's roof.

"I thought he was going to arrest me," Peter said.

"I wouldn't have let him," Gwen responded with a smile.

Peter liked Gwen. He also trusted her more than he trusted anyone else right now. "Gwen, I've been . . ." Peter began. "It's hard to know how to say it."

Gwen blushed. She thought he was talking about the two of them. She moved in close, and before he could say anything else, the two of them kissed.

Just then, Gwen's mom yelled for Gwen to come back into their apartment. Gwen's dad had to leave suddenly. There was trouble on the Williamsburg Bridge, and Captain Stacy had to investigate. But so did the Amazing Spider-Man.

When Gwen turned around, Peter Parker was gone. . . .

AS SPIDER-MAN, Peter Parker swung through the streets of New York on his way to the Williamsburg Bridge. As he neared Delancey Street, Peter felt a strange tingling sensation in his head. It was a premonition, a warning that something was wrong and that Peter was in danger. This was Peter's spider-sense, and it was tingling like crazy!

Suddenly, a car flew right off the bridge! Peter could see that the driver was still inside, screaming.

SPIDER-MAN HAD TO ACT FAST!

With no time to lose, Peter began shooting webs as quickly as he could. He fired one shot after another. *Thwip! Thwip! Thwip!* Soon, the car that had been knocked off the bridge was caught in a massive spider-web. Peter fired off more webs so that the car now dangled from the Williamsburg Bridge, suspended over the Lower East Side for all to see.

The driver was safe, but Peter's spider-sense was still tingling. He quickly swung away to investigate. He knew he had to get to the top of the bridge as fast as possible!

SPIDER-MAN ARRIVED ATOP the Williamsburg Bridge just in time to see something big and fast moving from one end to the other, knocking cars off as it went by. It was larger than a man and looked almost reptilian, but Peter would deal with it later. Right now, he had people to save!

A taxicab screeched to a halt as Spider-Man landed in front of it. A terrified woman screamed from the backseat. "There it is—that's the *thing* that did this!" she yelled.

The cab driver revved his engine and the car lurched forward. That's when Peter realized the woman was talking about him.

"Whoa! Hey! I'm on your side," Spidey said, but it was too late. The cab was now driving directly at him!

Spider-Man jumped high into the air and landed on the windshield of the cab. Peter moved to the hood, but this did nothing to calm down the cabbie or his passenger. Now they were both screaming for help. Peter did the only thing he could think of to settle their nerves.

Peter Parker took off his **SPIDER-MAN** mask.

"See?" Peter began. "Normal guy, right?" The cabbie and the passenger were relieved. "Now get to safety," Peter continued. "I don't know what caused this, but I don't want you here if it comes back!"

SPIDER-MAN SURVEYED THE SCENE ON THE BRIDGE. It was chaos. People were running in every direction, yelling and screaming. Others were calling relatives and others were even taking pictures of the destruction with their cell phones.

Then there were the cars. Some of them were dented, others were overturned, and others were precariously balanced on the edge of the bridge, as if the slightest movement would send them plunging into the depths of the East River below.

A sudden cry for help told Peter what he had to do first. A station wagon had been knocked upside down, with a family of four still inside. A fire had broken out in the engine and was quickly spreading to the rest of the car. There was no time to lose!

Peter raced over to the car and, using all of his might, shattered the rear window with a mighty blow. "Hey, it's the Spider-Guy!" the little boy in the backseat yelled. "I saw you on the Internet!"

"Um . . . hi," Peter said. "Let's get you guys out of there, then we can talk about my extracurricular activities." But the flames were too strong. They licked at Peter's arms as he reached for the family. It was time for plan B.

Peter aimed his web-shooters and fired one web-blast after another at the flames. Soon, there was so much webbing over the engine that the oxygen supply to the fire had been cut off. The fire was extinguished—science class had saved the day!

As the family escaped, Peter jumped back to the cab. It was now time to rescue the rest of the cars. . . .

WITH EXPERT PRECISION, Peter fired web-lines at each of the balancing cars. He then connected the webs to the bridge's suspension towers, so that the cars would not fall.

From there, Peter ran to each car and fired more web-lines so that any car dangling off the bridge had a makeshift web-ladder for the passengers to escape. That's when Peter saw the familiar red and blue flashing lights of the New York Police Department.

Captain Stacy had arrived on the scene and was headed straight for Spider-Man. Peter put his mask back on so Gwen's father wouldn't recognize him. It was time for him to leave.

Peter raced over the bridge toward the Brooklyn side. Then he heard a voice yell out to him. It was the little boy that Peter had saved from the burning station wagon. He was standing next to his parents and his sister, calling out. "Wait—what's your name?" he asked.

Spider-Man paused and looked from the family of four to the devastation on the bridge, to the New York skyline, and then back to the family.

"I'm Spider-Man," he said. Then he fired a web and swung off into the night. **AMAZING.**

PARKING
DO NOT BLOCK
ACTIVE DRIVEWAY

AS SPIDER-MAN SWUNG FROM BROOKLYN back to Aunt May's house in Forest Hills, Queens, he thought about everything that had happened to him recently.

Average teenager Peter Parker was now anything but average. He was the sensational, the spectacular, the Amazing Spider-Man. He had great power, and with great power came great responsibility.

It was a responsibility to use his powers for good—to help people in need. He also felt a responsibility to find Uncle Ben's killer and bring him to justice, and to make sure that a tragedy like that did not happen again.

Peter also felt a responsibility to be there for Aunt May. She had raised him since he was four years old, and she was now the only family he had left. He wouldn't let her down. Peter was going to prove that to her. He just needed to make one stop before he got home.

The next morning, Aunt May walked into the kitchen to make breakfast for Peter and herself. She felt tired from another sleepless night, but when she opened the fridge, her whole face lit up and she beamed with pride.

Inside the refrigerator were twenty cartons of eggs. Not only had Peter remembered, but he had gone above and beyond. Aunt May smiled and knew that everything was going to be all right.

PETER PARKER SCALED THE SKYSCRAPERS OF NEW YORK CITY as the Amazing Spider-Man. He knew that whatever had caused all that damage on the bridge was still out there, and it was his job—his responsibility—to find whoever or whatever had caused that destruction and stop it.

He knew that it wouldn't be easy, especially not with the police department convinced he was a menace. But he also knew that he had Aunt May and Gwen to rely on, and kids like the ones from the bridge who now looked up to him. All in day's work for your friendly neighborhood Spider-Man, Peter thought.

Underneath the mask, Peter Parker smiled.

THE END